STANLEY'S EGGS

Published by Crane Books in 2021

Crane Books Ltd
The Red House, 10 Market Square
Amersham, Buckinghamshire, HP7 0DQ, UK

Text and illustrations © Daryl Stevenson 2020

A CIP Catalogue Record of this title is available from the British Library

isbn: 978-1-911060-44-4

Printed in China

For Xavi
Our first little chick...
Love you all the way
to the stars and back!
G xxx

Stanley's Eggs

written and illustrated by Daryl

Stanley and his wife Amelia live on the beautiful island of MADAGASCAR

where they built
themselves a rather
splendid nest.

Stanley was
very proud...

because Amelia
had just laid...

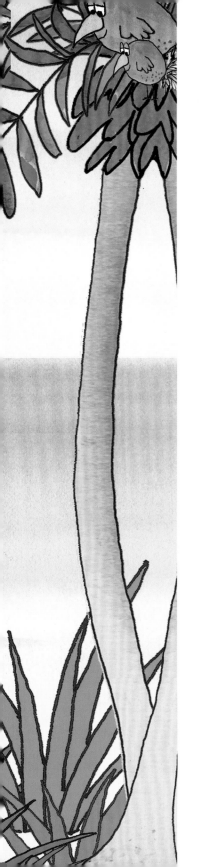

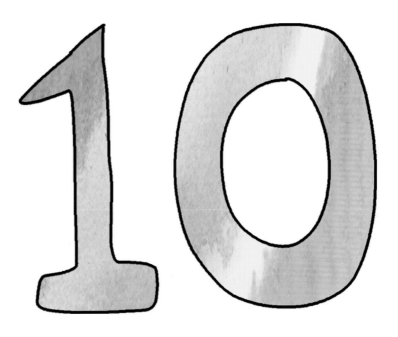

10

BEAUTIFUL EGGS!

Each egg was a
different color:

RED, YELLOW, ORANGE, TURQUOISE,

PINK, PURPLE, BLUE, GREEN, WHITE...

And a particularly beautiful rainbow colored one!

Amelia sat on the eggs day and night waiting patiently for them to hatch, until...

"Stanley, I have been sitting on these eggs for ages and you haven't sat on them once, so now it's your turn!"

Amelia picked up her handbag and flew off to do some shopping and have a bit of lunch,

while Stanley settled down on the eggs.

Everything seemed
very normal, until…

There was a very loud

CRACK

Stanley was thrilled!

There was one little pink chick staring at him.

Amelia was going to be so
pleased with his egg
sitting skills!

Then, one by one all the
other chicks appeared.

The blue one, the green one, the
pink, purple, and the orange one,
and then finally the white,
red, and turquoise.

Soon they were flying about and all over the place!

"STANLEY!
WHERE ARE OUR EGGS?"

(Amelia sounded very cross indeed)

1 2 3 4 5 6 7 8 9

"They're here, Amelia.
Come and see!

They are all here, look!"

"Stanley, one is missing.

Where is number ten?"

"I'm here!"

Squeaked a tiny voice,

"I'm stuck in the nest!"

Once the little chick had been helped out of the nest, Stanley counted them again…

1
2
3
4
5
6 7 8 9

Plus himself and Amelia,
that made twelve.
One big happy family!

10

It was a good thing that Amelia had gone shopping that day, because there was no time for shopping after that!

And as for Stanley, well he was very busy too because Amelia had just laid another

10

beautiful eggs!